For Alex
xx

The Bonkers Banana © 2014 by Allan Plenderleith
For more books by Allan visit www.allanplenderleith.com

First published in 2014

by

Ravette Publishing Limited
PO Box 876, Horsham, West Sussex RH12 9GH

ISBN: 978-1-84161-387-1

The Bonkers Banana

by Allan Plenderleith

ℛℛ
RAVETTE PUBLISHING

It was Christmas Eve and all was quiet,
as the snow fell gently like icing sugar on
a sponge cake.
Half way down the street was a house
which was about to receive a special visitor.

Santa!

This particular house had no chimney,
but not to worry, Santa knew what to do.
For the door had a keyhole, and that
was all he needed.

He used his special magic dust to
Shrink down
until he was really really small,
and float through the little keyhole.

But suddenly Santa bumped into
something - a rather empty bowl of fruit.
And his magic dust fell all over
something yellow and bendy.

A banana.

Then something magical happened.
The banana sprang to life!
"I'm alive! And I'm yellow! And bendy!
What am I? Maybe I'm a boomerang!"

The banana decided to find out if this was true by spinning around in circles and jumping in the air.
"Wheeee! Woohoooo! Waaahey!"

Meanwhile Santa looked worried.
"Oh no - all my magic dust is gone!
Without it I can't ride my sleigh or
deliver all the presents!"

But the banana who was COVERED in
magic dust, began to fly around the room!
"Wheeeeeeee! I AM a boomerang!"

Then the banana noticed sad Santa.
"Oh dear! Your smile is upside down
like me when I do this..."

" I know - we need more magic dust or
Christmas will be cancelled!" said Santa.

"Magic dust? Where does that come from?"
asked the banana.
"Well where ALL magic dust comes from
- the moon of course!"
"That's bonkers!" said the banana.

"Well if that's where it comes from
we have to fly up there and get some!"
said the banana. "But how?" said Santa.
"I'm covered in magic dust! You can fly on me!"
said the banana.

"That's bonkers, banana!"
said Santa.

"Bonkers banana! I like the sound of that!
All aboard the bonkers banana!"
said the bonkers banana.

And with that, Santa climbed aboard.
"Let's save Christmas!"

They flew out the letterbox and up into the night sky!
Wooohoooooooo!

But suddenly they bumped into something.
Something BIG. It was an alien spaceship!
"Aliens on Christmas Eve?
That's bonkers!" said Santa.

Two little aliens popped out.
They looked very grumpy.
"Oi! Get out of our way! We are in the
middle of taking over Planet Earth! Atchoo!!!"

"Gesundheit!" said the banana,
though he wasn't sure why.

"Why are your smiles on upside down?
They look like me when I do this."

"We are grumpy because our planet ATCHOO is covered in dust and makes us ATCHOO, sneeze all day ATCHOO long!"

"Planet Atchoo? I've never heard of that!"
said the banana.

"No! It's not called Planet Atchoo
- it's called the MOON!" said the alien.
And he pointed to a big banana-shaped
planet in the sky.

"Dust? On the moon?
But that's MAGIC dust!
That's what we need to save Christmas!"
said Santa excitedly.

"Well we can help you –
we'll clean the moon,
collect the magic dust,
save Christmas and the world!!"
said the banana.

"Mmm, that's bonkers!" said one of the aliens.
"But it just might work!"
And his smile wasn't upside down any more.

"Aliens - take us to your big banana in the sky!" said the bonkers banana.

And so Santa rode the banana
and the aliens flew their spaceship
all the way up to the
big banana in the sky.

Now that's something you don't see
every day.

They were almost at the moon
when Santa began to feel funny.
"Our magic dust...it's wearing off!"

Suddenly...

POP! Santa was his normal size!
The banana couldn't fly!
They fell towards the moon!

They lowered slowly to the dusty moon
and the aliens appeared.
"ATCHOO! Now you can see ATCHOO
the problem we have ATCHOO!"

The banana looked at the surface of the moon - it was COVERED in sparkly magic dust! "ATCHOO! Yes this IS dusty! ATCHOO!" sneezed the banana.

But then the banana had an idea.
"Santa - your present sack!
Can I look inside please?"
"Yes of course, but what for?" wondered
Santa.

The bonkers banana rummaged around and
pulled out a tiny toy vacuum cleaner.
Then he picked up some magic dust and
sprinkled it over the toy.

The banana jumped on, switched on the vacuum cleaner and WHOOSH off he went!

Wheeeeeeeeeeeeeee!!!

The aliens and Santa watched the banana
ride the vacuum cleaner all over the moon.

That's ANOTHER thing you
don't see every day!

Finally all the magic moon dust
had been gathered up
and the moon was shiny and bright.
Like a brand new banana!

But Santa looked worried.
"We only have five minutes left before
the first children begin waking up!
I don't think we can do it,
even with all the magic dust in the world."

Then the aliens had an idea.
"You can use our transporter ray to BEAM
all the presents straight into their homes!"

The alien pointed the ray gun at the
sack of presents and...

ZAAAAP!

...all across the world, under every good girl and good boy's Christmas tree appeared a big pile of presents!

"All thanks to you bonkers banana!"
said Santa.
"But don't forget there's one more present
left to deliver!" said the bonkers banana.
And he was right...

The next morning...

The End

Other titles by Allan Plenderleith

The Smelly Sprout

Why does nobody like me?

by Allan Plenderleith

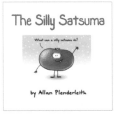

The Silly Satsuma

What can a silly satsuma do?

by Allan Plenderleith

The Christmas Carrot

Everyone wants a piece of me!

by Allan Plenderleith

The Boy Giant
by Allan Plenderleith

Available on the iPhone
App Store

kindle fire

The Chicken & the egg
by Allan Plenderleith

Princess Chocolate

Allan Plenderleith

Discover more at allanplenderleith.com